Moon Over Tennessee

Moon Over Tennessee

~ **A Boy's Civil War Journal** ~

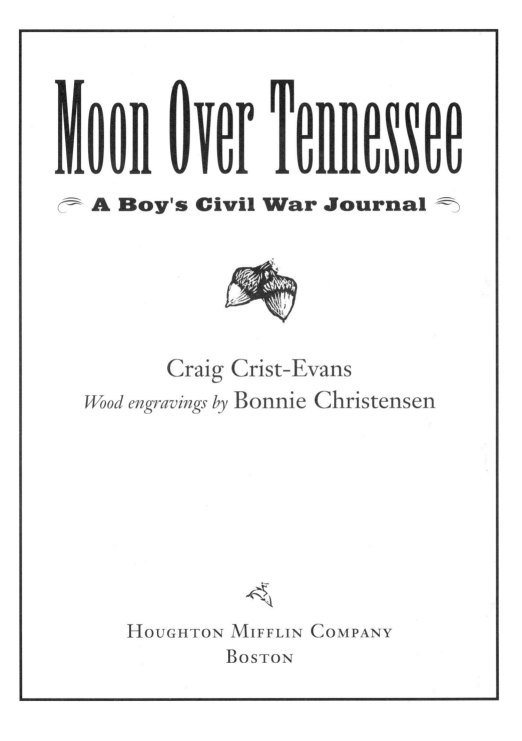

Craig Crist-Evans

Wood engravings by Bonnie Christensen

HOUGHTON MIFFLIN COMPANY

BOSTON

For Yann and Katie
—C. C.-E.

For Jan
—B. C.

Thank you to Special Collections and Research Annex of the Bailey Howe Library.

Text copyright © 1999 by Craig Crist-Evans
Illustrations copyright © 1999 by Bonnie Christensen

The text of this book is set in 11-point Janson.
The illustrations are wood engravings.

Library of Congress Cataloging-in-Publication Data

Crist-Evans, Craig.
Moon over Tennessee / Craig Crist-Evans ; illustrated by Bonnie Christensen.
p. cm.
Summary: A thirteen-year-old boy sets off with his father from their farm in Tennessee to join the
Confederate forces on their way to fight at Gettysburg. Told in the form of diary entries.
ISBN 0-395-91208-3
1. United States — History — Civil War, 1861–1865 — Juvenile fiction. [1. United States — History
— Civil War, 1861–1865 — Fiction. 2. Fathers and sons — Fiction. 3. Diaries — Fiction.] I.
Christensen, Bonnie, ill. II. Title.
PZ7.C869365Mo   1999
[Fic] — DC21   98-11912 CIP AC

Manufactured in the United States of America
RO 10 9 8 7 6 5 4 3 2

Moon Over Tennessee

April 24, 1863
Silver Bluff, Tennessee . . . leaving home

From the barn I see my mother on the back porch washing beans,
my little sister with her dolls there on the stoop, my father
leading horses from the field.

Morning sun crawls up, a yellow dog just waking,
stretching one leg and another, then
its wide-mouthed fiery yawn. I rub my eyes and push
my hand behind a plank, grope until my fingers
close around the edges of a wooden box. Crouched
down in the hay, I lift the top. *Nothing much*, I think,
worth anything to anyone but me: my grandpa's pocket knife,
the pin my mother wore before my baby brother died,
an arrowhead I found down by the creek. I touch each thing,
but hear my father's step and quickly put the knife into my pocket,
close the box and slip it back into its hiding place.

He stands inside the door, his hat pulled down, a bridle
hanging loosely in his hands. Behind him, sunlight
makes shadows dance across the dusty floor.
The valley out beyond our homestead opens like a picture,
fields of green splashed everywhere with flowers,
barns and houses tucked in nests of trees, cows
and horses bending to the young sweet grass.

I've lived here long as I remember,
carved into this family like my daddy's name
cut deep into the oak that stands
there at the corner of the field.

It's not because my daddy thinks
the South should fight against the North,
but we've been so long a piece of Tennessee,
today we're leaving for the war.

Pa waves me over to the horses. They stamp
and whinny softly, nuzzling me as I move near.
Old Jed, my favorite, nibbles at my sleeve.
Pa's red roan, Betty, backs away from the bridle,
nostrils flared, her head held high.

The sun climbs up above the poplars
standing like a row of bent old soldiers to the north.

I brush the horses down, spread blankets
on their broad, strong backs. Pa helps me
with the saddles, too big for me to lift myself.
When both of them are ready, we lash
our rucksacks filled with clothing, food and water.
Pa slides his rifle into a holster on the roan.

I think about my best friend John,
his dark eyes wise with the kind of pain that comes
from being black. My daddy says his daddy
got set free, but sometimes I can see
the chains still in his eyes.

John walks slowly from the fence that separates
their farm from ours. I try to speak
but don't know what to say.

Just past the fencerow, we turn the horses back
and wave at Ma, Little Sister, and John. The moon
is still a ghost above the hills of Tennessee.

April 30, 1863
Cumberland Valley, Virginia . . . on the road

Six days now riding north and I am scared.
The mountains and the valleys smell of dust and fire.
Clouds bank over mountains, then rain collects in gullies,
streaming down in dirty rivulets. Birds start nervously
from the gleaming branches of trees.

I miss my mother and my sister. I miss the woods,
the morning smell of cornbread in the oven,
and rain, the way it soaks into the rich black dirt.
I even miss the schoolhouse, gray and shabby,
standing in the middle of a field. John is not
allowed to go inside, but sometimes walks with me and waits,
Charley curled in the shade asleep, while John
listens at the window, scratching letters in the dirt,
counting numbers like the notes in some old song.

Pa says we'll meet the troops near Fredericksburg.
Far off in a valley I hear dogs. He doesn't say,
but I think my pa is scared as me.

Last night, I lay awake beneath the stars,
frogs and crickets singing deep inside the woods.

A Negro family crept across the clearing and,
when they saw us bedded down,
froze stone still outside the flickering light.

My pa woke up and grabbed his gun, but saw it wasn't
Federals and gave them water and a stack of hardtack
bigger than my fist.

I could see them talking, quiet by the fire.
Then the family disappeared into the night.

May 3, 1863
Fredericksburg, Virginia . . . training camp

When we get to camp, there's laughter and the sound
of stone on steel bayonets, a thousand voices
hollering and whispering and lifting up in song.
Old men and boys rush from one place to another,
most dressed in ragged coats and worn-out shoes,
country hats pulled down around their ears.

I think of Little Sister and the chickens
and the long, thick rows of sorghum
that will be sprouting soon.

I imagine tiny seeds Ma presses in the ground,
each one asleep until the rain and sun grow warm
and the seed-shell cracks. Then a finger of a root
begins to push into the earth.

By the time I get back home, the fields will be
woven thick with leaves. I ask Pa how long
we will be gone. He shakes his head and smiles,
but it's not the kind of smile makes me happy.

I wish I knew what he was thinking, his eyes
like stones beneath his brow.

Last year, he took me hunting. Before we left
he pulled a box out of the kitchen trunk. I could see
him proud and happy as he handed it to me.
"Open it," he said, and I pried loose the slats
and brushed away wood shavings till I saw
the gun — blue steel shining in the lantern light.
I couldn't say a word, but gently lifted it and put it
to my shoulder, felt the heft of it, the smoothness
of the polished stock. That day, I shot a rabbit
and Pa bent like prayer above the body,
showing me the way to cut it down the belly,
how to gut it with a quick swipe of the hand.

May 6, 1863
Fredericksburg, Virginia . . . news of Chancellorsville

The camp is loud and dusty; must be a thousand men
marching to the beating drums, singing field songs. I watch
Jed and Betty while my pa learns how to duck and shoot
and roll and hide inside the dry tall grass.

There's talk of Chancellorsville.
All day, soldiers have been pouring in.
One with bloody bandages around his head
stumbles to our tent and begs a drink.

He whispers, "Left 'em runnin'," voice hoarse with dust.
"They's talk Lee wants to push to Pennsylvania now."

My daddy's bent above a pot of coffee steaming on the fire.
He stands and hands a ladle to the boy, no more than seventeen,

and points him to the water wagon down the line.
"How many dead?" Pa asks.

"Don't know. No way to tell.
So many cannon throwing grape and canister,
the lines broke time and time again,
but then we held."

May 18, 1863
Fredericksburg, Virginia . . . thinking of home

At night we gather by the fires.
A boy named Seth is camped beside us with his pa.
He says he's from Atlanta and asks about our farm.
I tell him how the moon comes up above the old gray barn,
corn swaying in the night like dancers painted white.

I tell him how at dusk I go down to the creek
that drops out of the hills and winds through gullies
till it reaches Muddy Pond. I can tell he's never
been out to the country, so I tell him in the best voice
I can find,

"I stand as still as Jesus on the Cross and wait
until a crawdad scuttles from a rock,
then flash my hands into the water. I never miss.
John and me gig frogs in summer too."

I can tell he wishes he could visit by the way his eyes get far away.

"When the war is done," I tell him, "walk until the hills
look just like heaven. Then you'll know
you've made it up to Tennessee."

May 25, 1863
Fredericksburg, Virginia . . . on the move

This morning is a whirlwind, men and horses
racing through the camp. Last night they sent down
orders for us to cross the Blue Ridge into Shenandoah.

Pa and I load Jed and Betty, pack bedrolls,
pots and food. Everywhere, men hitch wagons
to the big draw horses, set cannon for the march.

Seth has his daddy's horse all saddled up when I come by.
He's pale and his eyes are big. He looks at me
as though he's never seen my face before.

May 29, 1863
Near Brandy Station, Virginia . . . marching

It's hard to breathe and hard to move, soldiers
pushing from behind, the air a bowl of dust.

A man walking next to Pa grabs his stomach,
stumbles, and is shoved aside. I hear him moan,
then someone stops and offers him some water.

I'm so hungry I could eat the dirt by noon, but Pa
hurries me along. By two, I think I'm dying,
and then I hear a voice above the rumble of our marching
call out, "Halt!"

We find a patch of shade beneath an oak and lean
against the rough old bark to eat.
Pa hands me hardtack, pork, a canteen full of water.

I close my eyes and imagine John
marching here beside me, that dark,
sad strength like steel running up his spine.
For all the hurt the world's tossed him and his pa —
his mama dead, his brother whipped so bad
he sits all day and rocks — I sometimes think
if I was John I'd pack a horse and ride until I ran
clear out of people, just me and mountains and fields of grass
stretched as big as oceans toward the falling sun.

Pa lifts my hat and I know that I've been sleeping.
Everything is stiff and sore.
The resting's harder than the moving.
When we start to march again,
my feet feel bigger than my shoes.

The road begins to rise, and far off
I can see a smoky line of mountains.

When we stop to camp, I brush the horses down
and hobble them and give them sugar. "Sweet Betty,"
I whisper. "Good Jed." They like to hear my voice,
and nuzzle me and scratch themselves against a fallen pine.

The sun is fading west, and I can see
Blue Ridge peaks like sleeping giants disappear.

June 8, 1863
Brandy Station, Virginia . . . reviewing the cavalry

The camp is bristling with excitement.
General Lee is coming on the train today, and we
head down to the station. In the distance
a rope of thick black smoke bends back
along the body of the train.

The train coughs and slows. It stops and everyone is silent.
Then, the doors of a single car fly open and out steps Lee,
white hair long and blowing. I've never seen a general before.
He's not too tall, but stands as stiff as sabers raised up in salute.

There's talk Jeb Stuart's got his cavalry
drilled and ready for parade. I'm not supposed to,
but I sneak down to the riverbank and hide
where I can watch the horsemen ride.

Arranged in groups of four, they form a line that's miles long.
The General rides along, inspecting them, and nods his head,
then turns his horse and climbs a hill above the river.
Bugles sound and suddenly the whole brigade is prancing.

A storm of fine red dust rises where the horses turn and gallop.
I'm close enough to see their eyes, like proud deep wells,
and hear them champing on their steel bits.

The soldiers sit tall and straight. They yank the reins until
the bugles blow again and everything grows still.

From the hill, Lee lifts his shining sword,
then the horsemen start to move again,
slowly as they cross the field.

I slip through trees and run until I find my pa.
I can't explain the way it makes me feel.
"You should have seen them riding," I say to him,
sucking breath in short, quick beats.
"It was like a dance, and no one missed a step."

He nods, but I know his mind is somewhere
off in Tennessee, dreaming of the corn in even rows,
Ma stirring mush until it bubbles on the iron stove,
Little Sister with her eyes squinched like the teacher
at the schoolhouse doing numbers
while she draws a picture she will keep for Pa.

June 9, 1863
Brandy Station, Virginia . . . surprise attack

Morning comes in shades of gray.
As if I dream it, there are gunshots,
bugle calls, and screaming. I sit up fast,
but Pa is up already, busy
pulling on his boots, his rifle
cocked and loaded on his cot.

Outside is still a dream, a nightmare.
Men are running everywhere, some fastening
shirts and trousers as they grab their horses' reins.

The guns are louder now, the smell of powder fills the air.
Our horses strain against the tethers. I try to calm them,
but they stamp their hooves and throw their great heads back.

Pa comes running and mounts his roan.
"Stay here and don't let no one near old Jed.
Soon as I am able, I'll be back."

Through the morning men stagger back to camp,
some moaning, barely standing, some
with stains of blood across their sweaty shirts.
One man jerks from his horse and then lies motionless.

The fighting slows by afternoon, but Pa has not come back.
I ask the others as they lead their horses by, or stumble
tired toward the tents, but no one knows a thing.

Just as the light begins to dim, I see him
moving toward me through the broken lines of men.

June 10, 1863
Culpeper Court House, Virginia . . . crossing the Cumberland

We move out slow, the air like wet sheets
steaming in the sun. No one talks except
to curse a blistered foot. Last night we watched
the lorries trundle in to load the sick and wounded
and carry them to Fredericksburg. I've never heard
that kind of wailing, like the dead, the way the preacher
says they're screaming down in Hell.

The march is slow through mountains hunched
between the valleys of the Cumberland and Shenandoah.
Walls of trees stretch miles toward the sky.
Even while I'm walking, my mind drifts off:

I'm working in the field and feel the train of summer
like an engine bearing down, its steady quiet
pounding the earth, corn exploding
all around, a sound of water in the distance.
John is running from the barn, a letter in his hand.
Charley follows, bouncing up and down between the rows.

John gives the letter to my father, who opens it
the way my mother turns sheets down on the bed,
slow and careful, patting down the corners as he pulls
the leaf-thin paper from the envelope. Pa's face grows
still and I can feel the air between us change. He
looks at me and puts an arm across my shoulder.
"It's your ma's pa, son. I gotta go and tell her.
You head back and get the buggy hitched."

Then I'm conscious of the war again and marching,
and I drag my sleeve across my face. That night,
when Grandpa died, I went out to the barn and dug
a cave inside the hay. John found me there,
my knees tucked up against my chin,
not knowing what to make of death.
"They's little deaths and big ones," he said to me.
"The little ones are happenin' all the time — the flowers,
grass, and crawdads — but the big ones, well, the big ones
touch you here." And he pointed to my heart.

As we climb, the nights grow cool,
the Milky Way is bright as winter moonlight on the farm.

June 19, 1863
Ashby's Gap, Virginia . . . crossing the mountains

Trees stretch thick across the Shenandoah Valley.
Far below, a river snakes, sunlight
flashing on its silver scales.

Step by step, stone by slippery stone,
the horses pick their way along a creek.

Pa walks slowly beside his Betty. "Son," he says,
"I don't know where we're going, what's gonna happen,
but you got to promise me a thing. No matter what . . ."

He hesitates and looks me in the eye. I step
around a boulder planted smack dab in the middle
of the path. I feel shaky when he's serious like this.

"Just promise me you'll get back home and help your ma.
She's got a lot to think about. She'll need a man."

I'm watching where the water disappears beneath
big, mossy stones and shadowed roots of trees.
I feel the tears before they show. I can't look up.
I know a man don't cry, but here I go.
Out of nowhere a picture of our farm
emerges from a fog. I see the hawk I watched
last summer, circling lazy over granite cliffs.
It seems to hang above one spot, then,
in an instant, dives and arcs back up,
a black snake swinging from its talons.

"Pa," I say, the word sounds choked. "Pa,
ain't nothin' gonna happen."

I can't see the valley anymore. Hickory and sweet gum
grow so close it's dark before the sun is gone. A clearing opens up
where we unload the animals and cut dry wood for fires.

By nightfall camp's secured; sentries posted every twenty feet,
camp dogs curled near the fires. I think of Charley,
dreaming about rabbits, twitching in his sleep.

I hear an owl who I think watches everything
around the world drifting off.

"Pa," I ask him just before we sleep,
"do you think it's right, what we are doing?"

He looks across at me, darkness like a weight
between our eyes. "There's nothing right with killin'."
His voice is soft and then he's still.

I lie awake a long time, listening to the owl.
Hoo! Hoo! he says. Crickets answer
with their steady buzz. A wind leafs through the trees,
soft as Mama's hands against my cheek.

June 29, 1863
Chambersburg, Pennsylvania . . . waiting

Pa says the Union troops in Gettysburg are volunteers
and couldn't whip a churn of butter. Tomorrow,
he and some others plan to raid
a factory where they make shoes.

It's been so long since I had good shoes,
I don't know if my feet will want to wear them.

Tonight we sleep in a grassy meadow. The ground
is cool, the stars a hazy curtain in the sky.

June 30, 1863
Chambersburg Pike . . . battle

Not long after dawn I hear shots fired.
Pa rushes into camp and hurries me to get the horses.
I pull my shirt on, grab my pack, and run
like lightning for the horse corral.

As we creep along the Pike, there's something
moving everywhere. When the wind blows down the grass,
Pa swings his rifle wide and aims. A wild turkey
scares up from a huckleberry bush, a blur of wings,
a *whoosh* not two feet overhead.

Now we're climbing. Soldiers lie in twos and threes
along the ridgeline, others falling out behind them,
loading rifles, pointing toward the valley, shooting.
The ground is torn and blistered.

The sound is louder than it was at Brandy Station.
I think the air is one big cannon booming.

Now men are streaming down as we go up,
bleeding, crying, calling names of friends and women
they left at home. I see a boy my age with rags
tied tight around his arm, soaked
bright red and dripping.

July 2, 1863
Seminary Ridge, West Side . . . close to Gettysburg

Today, the air is like a drum, beating out
the cries of dying soldiers, North and South.

Fields are so drenched with blood you can't stand up
except to slip again and fall.

Down by the creek the wounded lie in rows
like pine logs at the mill in Silver Bluff.
Working up the gutted ridge, we file by them.

Water stands in bloody pools; no one goes near
though their tongues are black with thirst.

July 3, 1863
Seminary Ridge, East Side . . . Seth's father dies

Men and horses swirl in a panic.
Cannon shot sprays dirt in all directions.
Bullets whistle through the air.

By now, the sun has baked the ground to brick,
horses huddle in what shade has not been blown away.
Grass is withered even where it's not torn up and burnt.

My pa comes back for water, then disappears
again into the raging storm of bullets.

I know enough to think of something good.
I squinch my eyes and see my ma:
she's singing in the field back behind the barn,
the sun a golden coin above the hills.

Seth sits down and leans against a ragged tree.
His eyes are blank and aimed somewhere inside.
"My pa is dead," he says. "They shot him right in front of me."

I can't imagine what he's thinking, or if he's thinking
anything at all. I try to give
him water and a piece of jerky, but
he doesn't even look at me.

I say his name. A breeze comes up and blows
the words like feathers toward the trees.

"Even when the cannons quit," he says,
"I can hear them pounding in my ears."

July 4, 1863
Gettysburg, Pennsylvania,
near Cemetery Hill . . . shock and prayer

I'm crouched behind an ancient oak.
Boys my age and men are screaming.
Some lie broken in the grass, smoke
rolling up like clouds among the trees.
Three days of fighting now, and I don't understand
why we came to fight this Yankee war.

Some say it's for the slaves,
but I don't think that's true.

Pa's said a hundred times that no one
really owns another human being.

But what owned *him* took him like a snap —
a trigger and a leaden slug.

Who owns him now?
And what of me?
I hold my hands like flags against the sky.
Dirty, rough, they wave there, and I am
more afraid right now than I have ever been.

This morning, while the soldiers fought their last retreat,
I saw him stand up in the meadow down by the bloody creek.
He stood and spun as if someone had punched him in the face.

When I got to him, he couldn't say my name.
He raised a hand to touch my cheek,
a kind of sadness in his eyes, no words, and then
his hand fell back into the dust.

All day the guns continued to explode, cannon pounding too.
Grapeshot strafed the trees and I wrapped blistered arms
around my knees, rocking till the moon began to rise.

Night now, and the corpsmen move among the bodies.
They lift them up and carry them away. I listen
to them grunting with the weight and watch
their lanterns bob like boats across the hills.

In the morning, smoke hangs like oil in the valley.

July 5–9, 1863
Gettysburg, Pennsylvania . . . turning back

I pack some food and blankets on the roan
and ride Jed south along the Shenandoah,
toward the forests of the Cumberland.

I'm numb and riding slow.
The horses seem to know that Pa is gone.
They roll their eyes and shake their heads and whinny.

I think about the moon that comes up buttery and big
above the sorghum fields, my mama singing softly
as the stars come out. How can I tell her Pa is gone?
She'll hurt until the hurt is bigger than the sky.

From Pennsylvania through the valleys of Virginia,
men creep like shadows along the roads.

Women bend in gardens near small houses,
kneel by their children.

Young girls wash soldiers' shirts in rivers.

My father's dead, and I will have to tell my mother
I watched him die.

I stop at night and listen to the big sky whisper,
make my camp and build small fires just to keep the dark at bay.

My third night out, I think I hear my father in the wind.
His voice is soft. I rise up from the log where I've been sitting
and take my grandpa's knife out of my pocket.
There, surrounded by the grass and trees, insects
like a thousand army drummers keeping beat,
I carve my daddy's name into a tree.

John will ask what Pennsylvania looked like.
I'll tell him it was dark, too dark to see.

July 10, 1863
Leaving the Shenandoah Valley, Virginia . . . the long ride

Everywhere, the song of slaves is whistling.
But the words are new. They sing of freedom,
and smooth black faces smile
from open doors and windows. Children
chase each other across fields, into thick,
dark woods and down to streams.

When magnolia blossoms start to hang their scented heads,
and the mountains of the Cumberland stretch out,
I know my home is near, and think again
about the moon that comes in at my window,
bathing Little Sister's face and stealing silently across
the rough wood floor until it pours like syrup
up the table's legs, sprawls across the chairs and reaches
daguerreotypes hung there along the wall:

grandfathers, grandmothers, cousins standing stiff,
surrounded by magnolia trees and dogwoods
all different shades of brown.

July 15, 1863
South of Fredericksburg, Virginia . . . a dream

Now everywhere, I smell the sun upon the land,
the good clean sweat of farms. Cows
like lazy villagers look up, then drop their heads
into the tall thick grass and chew,
tails flicking flies.

In a dream, cicadas make a song like knives
being sharpened on the world's stone.

A honeysuckle moon hangs over everything,
while soldiers rise up from the ground at Gettysburg.

One by one and two by two they stand.
They crane their necks and stare into the gentle light
that fills the sky like rain, that paints the field white.

I wake and realize none of them
will ever ride back home to see the stars
come up above the homes they left.
My father will not smell the sweet magnolia
or the muddy river breath; he will not
hear the meadowlark at dawn.

July 22, 1863
Cumberland Mountains, Virginia . . . sadness everywhere

The owl says nothing as I ride.

The fox lies still beside the road.

Dogs on porches raise themselves on tired paws
and cock their ears and bay and curl up again to sleep.

The moon moves east to west and I am lonely,
but I sit up in the saddle and remember
songs my pa would sing me
while we hayed or brought in corn.

Towns and cities seem to shiver: broken
windows, burned-out homes, and wagons
straining shoulders of old horses.

Some people say hello, their voices cracked and heavy.
Others crouch by sawdust fires, silent
as the night cups chilly hands around them.

Above it all the clouds march noiselessly.

The country sleeps and wakes.

I wonder how the other families without fathers,
without sons, will take the plow back up,
will bring the cows at dusk to drink, will tuck
the babies into beds and say, "Sweet dreams."

July 28, 1863
Silver Bluff, Tennessee . . . coming home

Finally, the hills become familiar.
Lights emerge from trees like fireflies.
The road is rutted, dry and hot,
even though the night is cool.

Faint voices and the quiet *hoo!* of owls
and the chatter of a squirrel and of water
tumbling over stones all weave together
and I begin to cry, but it is different now.
I don't know how to say it, but I am *glad*.
These tears are like a grieving washing out of me.

From the window of a small brown house,
a child's laughter pours into the night.

Down this road and up another hill, then from the crest
I see the valley where my family lives,
where I was young three months ago,
where cats slink warily from house to barn,
tobacco leaves hang drying from the beams,
where Little Sister pulls the covers up
and lets her head drop back into the pillow,
where John holds Charley in a wild dream,
where Mama banks the fire, sweeps the floor,
pulls curtains over windows, and steps
for one last look onto the porch.

She's standing there as I ride up, the shadows
of two horses and a boy, my hat pulled low, my eyes
dark rings, the reins like broken arrows in my hands.

Perhaps she thinks she sees a man ride up,
dismount, and tie his horse.

She stands as still as death and lets the moon erase
the shadows one by one, her right hand to her heart,
the other leaning hard against the rail.

I think she knows that I am home.

Perhaps she thinks I'm ghost or dream, but now
the moon lifts above the trees and I can see
her face as clearly as if day had turned around
and hurried back to welcome me.

The moon rises now above the barn,
shining on my face, and Ma lets out a sigh.

We don't say anything, just watch the eerie
landscape shiver in the pewter glow.

I want to tell her everything, but can't find words.
Instead of anything about the war, about my father dying,
I say, "I rode from Gettysburg to Tennessee
and I saw the country weeping."

In the morning, I will visit John.

At first, we won't know what to say,
the sun like pure molasses sticking to our skin,
the buzz of katydids, the trill of meadowlarks,
the little sound the creek makes tripping
over stones and mossy broken branches.

In the morning, I will visit John and call out Charley's name.

He'll run and jump on me, and John and I
will put our arms around each other's shoulder
the way we did when we were young.

I'm thirteen and I'm tired. All I want to do
is lie down in the bed my ma will make for me,
to sleep and dream of planting and of harvest,
to listen to the creek and take my little sister for a walk.

But I stand here with my mother on the front porch
watching clouds drift through the night like birds.
When she takes my hand in hers, I'm surprised how soft
it feels against my old rough palms and calloused fingers.

"I've come home to keep a promise," I say to her.
My voice just like my father's voice inside my head.
She nods. We watch the moon until it's high
above the cornrows and the woods beyond.

From Silver Bluff to Gettysburg

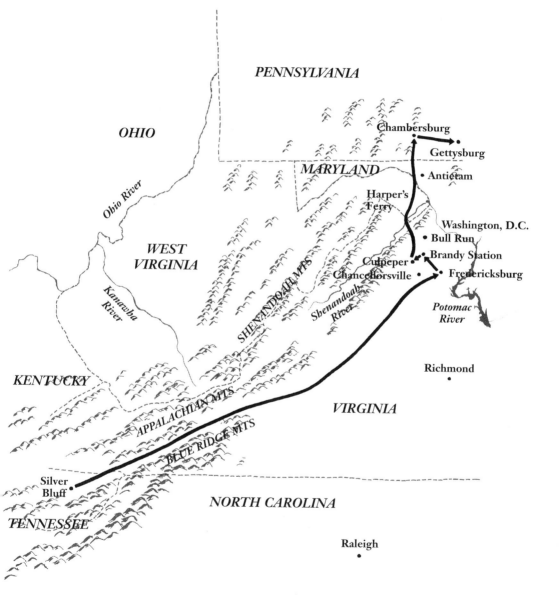

Afterword

Throughout the spring of 1863, Confederate and Federal forces skirmished along various fronts in Virginia. From Fredericksburg to Chancellorsville to Brandy Station, the war swept through the countryside. Ragged troops on both sides watched the perimeters of their encampments anxiously, never knowing when the enemy would appear like a ghost, rising up and streaming over ridges, emerging from thickets and woods, guns roaring, flags waving wildly in the rush to battle.

With the striking exceptions of Fredericksburg and Chancellorsville, which were victories for the South, few of the battles were decisive. Confederate General Robert E. Lee and Union General George G. Meade were both searching for an opportunity to turn the tide of the war. The South sought international support for its cause, and it needed the fresh sources of supplies a strategic victory would provide. President Lincoln was desperate for success, as political pressure was mounting against him.

After much thought and counsel, and emboldened by the victory at Chancellorsville, Lee decided to take the war into the North's own backyard. By invading the rich farming country of southern Pennsylvania, he reasoned, the South might drive fear into the hearts of the northern farmers and towns-folk—who had until then been relatively insulated from the main action of the war—and gain access to much-needed supplies of food and clothing.

On the morning of July 1, the handful of Southern troops moving into the town of Gettysburg had plans to raid a shoe factory and replace their worn-out boots. They did not guess that the most decisive battle of the war was about to begin. As they approached the town, they encountered a few advance Northern troops along the Chambersburg Pike, and shots were fired. Both sides retreated, but those few early-morning shots began a bloody engagement that would rage for three days and result in the retreat of the Confederate forces, beaten and humbled, back into Virginia. During those three days, more than 50,000 people from both sides were killed or wounded.

Following Gettysburg, the Federal army regrouped. That autumn, they mounted a fierce campaign at Chickamauga in Tennessee, and a month later broke through the lines of Confederate troops surrounding them at Chattanooga. From Chattanooga, the Federals had a clear path to Atlanta, and from Atlanta Sherman marched to the sea, burning everything in his path. Although the fighting dragged on for nearly two more years, Gettysburg is considered the turning point in a war that divided the United States, pitting brother against brother in the bloodiest conflict in American history.

Early in the war it was considered entertainment for the elite of Washington to come out in picnic dress to battlefields like Bull Run to watch the armies clash. In the evening, as the fighting slowed, men, women and children, on horses and in elegant coaches, would return to the city, and to peaceful sleep. But theirs was not the common experience. Throughout the war, it was not unusual to see young boys in the camps of both armies. Toward the end, so badly decimated were the ranks of available fighting-age men from the South, Confederate soldiers as young as twelve and thirteen were captured in battle.

In *Moon Over Tennessee* the narrator does not fight, but rides with his father to care for the horses and help with camp responsibilities. Though he doesn't bear arms, he finds himself in the middle of ferocious fighting and, ultimately, in the middle of a personal tragedy that brings the war to an awful conclusion for him and his family. How many boys went home to do the work of the men who would never return? It is a question that cannot be answered. We can only guess, and feel the terrible weight of war on their young shoulders.